Dancing on my catalyst

Written and illustrated by

J.R-Yeo

Dancing on my catalyst

By J.R-Yeo

Cover design by J.R-Yeo

Book design by J.R-Yeo

Printed by IngramSpark UK

Printed worldwide.

ISBN 978-1-7393238-0-6

Dancing on my catalyst

Contents – Art

Contents – Poetry

Dedicated to my mum... your storytelling felt like magic to me!

Mum, you carried our baton with great strength and pride. Never putting it down to rest... not once!

I do not have such astounding strength in my arms. But I will help to carry our baton with all that I have.

Not just for me... but for you too!

Introduction

This book is so called, because I successfully found positive ways to cope when my dad passed away.

Overwhelmed and numb, my mind was at tipping point. I realised that I needed to take steps to function and feel 'normal' again.

Sadly, there is no 'one size fits all' approach to navigating how to deal with bereavement. But writing poetry and drawing became my 'therapy' of choice. For me, I found it to be wholly immersive. I could transport a part of my mind to realms where, for a fraction of time at least, I escaped some of the pain. It gave me back some control to calm my mind.

Unable to talk about my emotions, writing gave me an outlet to pour out my pain and leave some of it there, on the page. It all started when I wanted to talk to my dad and tell him how I was feeling. His loss, a major catalyst, had left me so disorientated and empty. And so, I began to put my feelings down…

The poem 'How I feel' (pg. 66–69) is that very poem that I wrote to my dad in 2003.

Although the healing process was by no means quick, I remember feeling a sense of relief, solace even, as I took up my pencil or pen. No longer were my thoughts swimming around and drowning me in the chaos of my pain… but, a part of me was set free to roam. That part of me went to my 'happy place', where the world stopped still, allowing me to breathe and unravel and take a step forwards.

The poetry in this book may be about mundane things, but I never attempted to control this process. Thus, allowing the process to be unrestrained… organic. So, that whatever popped into my head, however ridiculous, I wrote about it or drew it. In turn, this aided my mind to unravel and let go of the abundance of 'thoughts'… I had a clear-out!

Some of my artwork 'tree people', so called by my children, were inspired in part by the wood grain on my laminated floor. If you stare long enough your mind makes up patterns… So, I drew what my mind saw.

Although my poetry and corresponding artwork are mostly unrelated to each other, they are all products of my personal journey to better mental health. Realising that this process was helping me, I was able to find acceptance, inner peace… and clarity!

So, in a world where we share ideas and experiences, this is mine that I share with you!

J.R-Yeo

Mother and baby

Rock me

I need someone to rock me,
Like a baby tucked up so warm.

Be snuggled tight within their arms,
As cradled, when first born.

Nothing else seems to matter...
...when I'm held so tight.

Makes all my fears just go away...
...disappear into the night.

Sing a lullaby to lull me.
I feel loved and fall asleep.

Then I can dream, a beautiful dream,
to replace the sadness that I keep.

For us
(Mid-2002–2003 and New Year 2004)

Before last Christmas was the start of our pain,
That would hit us time and time again!

Last New Year started as it intended to go on,
Taking our dearest loved ones, one by one.

This Christmas we try filling our hearts with hopeful glee,
But sadness it must still oversee.

This New Year we need to soldier on,
But our hearts hold tightly to the year just gone.

Where there is faith there cannot be pain!
Let our hearts smile, knowing in time we will see them
once again!

Feeling overshadowed

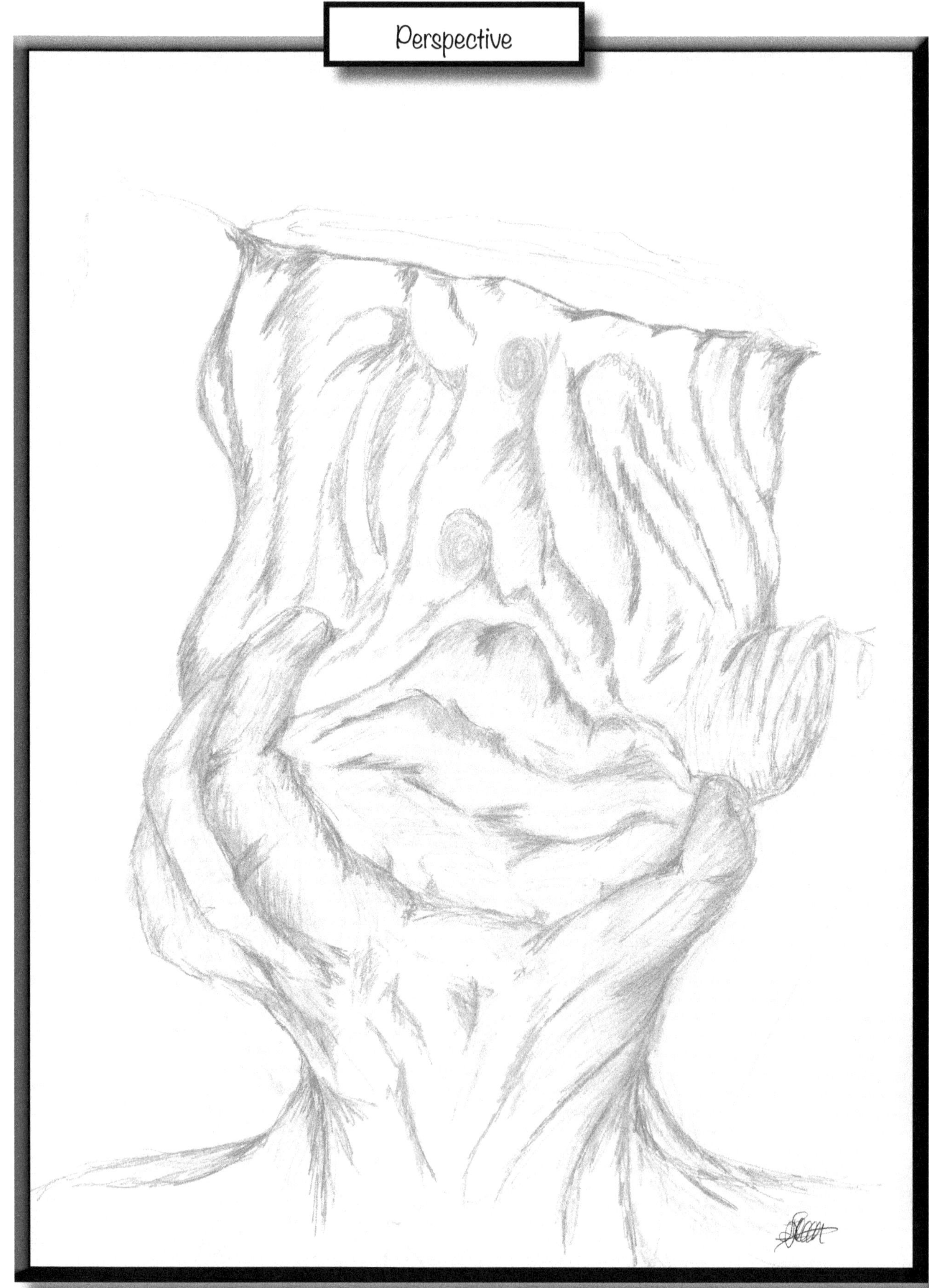

My thinking throne

I sit on my toilet, it's my thinking throne.
The kids try to disturb me, I scream, "LEAVE ME ALONE!"

The only place I get peace and calm, and no distress.
Sometimes I go sit there, just for a rest.

My very own thinking throne is second to none.
I am in heaven from sitting there, just scratching my bum.

Many a solution thought out at my little retreat.
Planned my wedding, my garden, and meals for my family to eat!

All the equipment I need is already there,
Just me, a full bog roll, and my thinking chair.

Some are sickened that I still sit when I am all done.
And say I should get up and go wipe my bum.

Great solutions to my problems just seem to appear,
As I leave no stone unturned, when I am sat thinking here.

That's why I'm not bothered, when emptied and fully drained...
That I continue to sit there, thinking all the same.

So modest, so placid, receptive... never moans.
So special, much needed, that's My Thinking Throne!

Survival... our greatest fight!

DEEP IN A DARK FOREST

Deep in a dark forest, I was all alone.
There wasn't anyone around, or even a phone!

It was dark, damp and gloomy, I barely could see.
Only the twilight glistening, to guide me through the tall trees.

I looked up, from where I lay, in some sort of spell.
How did I get here? I didn't know… wish someone could tell.

My body lay cushioned on leaves… fallen in the forest.
Had I been kidnapped? Left to die? My mind wouldn't rest.

The forest was enchanting, yet hostile to those new.
Watched on by the underworld, hoping to get you!

"What's that noise?" I jumped to my feet, terrified.
I tried to hide, then grasped my mouth… petrified.

My body hunched over; I stood dripping wet.
My face full of terror. I swung hysterically, right and then left.

My feet, aching and cold, squelched deep in the mud.
My body shaking, shivering, now chilled was my blood.

I heard a rustling, getting nearer, it was getting too close!
Nothing there! Was it my mind playing tricks? Was it a ghost?!

Animals of the forest around but keep out of sight.
Their reflective pupils twinkled, there in the night.

Walking slowly, I flinched, as branches wisped across my face.
Like an old lady's fingers tickling… made my heart race.

I heard a terrifying cackle, it was loud, evil and mean.
Maybe it wasn't a tree, after all, touching me.

The howling and wailing getting louder, I tried to retreat.
In panic, I stumbled, then crawled with my hands and my feet.

The pungent smells of the trees and animals filled the air.
Made me more scared for my life, I had to get out of here!

Out of breath, panting heavy, I got up… ran to an endearing light.
Turning my head frantically, running, hoping to make it alright.

There in front of me stood sanctuary, an old rickety house.
Weather-beaten with cobwebs, but I thought I was safer in, than out.

I stood, out of breath, looking down at my bedraggled clothes.
Badly ripped, they hung pitifully against my cold bones.

In trepidation I knocked at the door… it creaked… opening wide.
I stretched my neck forward and peered deep inside.

Then, from behind me, someone grabbed my shoulder real hard.
I did not wait to see who it was, I just hollered aaarrrrgggghhhhhhhh!

My heart pounding… Ba-boom! Ba-boom! I ran away… fast!
But then… my eyes opened wide… as I awoke from my dream… At last!

ROAR!

Office 'geek'

He sits alone at his desk. Tensely, he shifts in his chair.

Coyly, he smiles… says, "Good morning." Nobody answers… nobody dares!

No change, always feeling dejected, he gets back to work.

He doesn't have the courage to speak up and call them all 'jerks'.

For it would be a true crime, to communicate with the office geek.

Only to become an outcast yourself… excluded… considered a freak!

As they chat and laugh loud as they work, he starts to fantasise,

About a world where he fits in, feels wanted… feels alive!

He re-assembles his glasses, then shifts nervously in his chair,

Smiles awkwardly, but he's not stupid; he knows that they stare.

They only talk to him to poke fun… just for a laugh.

Find it amusing, when he looks up all excited, because he's finally asked.

Lonely heart has he, he works hard to get through each day.

Boss picks on him constantly, to boost his own ego. NOT okay!

No one will befriend him; he's so different from the rest.

Old-fashioned clothes, his hair – well, his mum tries her best!

He walks away, unwanted, from the office, with head bowed.

At functions, he's ignored, not allowed to join in with the 'in crowd'.

It's a shame that one's exterior means so much more; it's almost a sin.

When the true crux of a person, is held much deeper, in their soul within.

Well, he began to believe that it was 'he' unworthy of 'them'.

But by just skimming the surface, it was them losing out on knowing the true him!

If you're not attractive, slim, young, right colour or dressed in modern gear,

You may be placed on the outskirts, marginalised from your peers.

He had lots to offer, but they made him feel scared, always calling him a freak.

But people can be shallow, ignorant, cruel, when they look surface deep.

He looked down towards his feet as he spoke subservient in their face.

As if, just for speaking to them, he was a sickening disgrace.

One day, the boot will be on the other foot, the tables always get turned.

So just listen, take heed, from what can be learned.

They all rejected sitting near him, commented about a putrid smell.

Complained to the boss about him, made jokes and laughed loud as hell.

They sprayed air freshener in his presence, to embarrass him more.

It worked well, his sadness grew deeper, and he smiled coyly no more.

The boss called him to the office, warning him to have a wash.

He never returned to the office again, instead he just vanished!

That day, he walked alone at lunch, bought a packet of crisps.

Never to be seen again in the office after that, or even sadly missed!

Those ignorant office staff thought they had triumphed, done well.

When a week later they had all been informed that he was very unwell.

He held a secret, beneath his smile, where more than sadness lay.

He'd had skin cancer for years; neither the smell nor the cancer would ever go away.

He gave up the will to fight, soon passed away from his disease.

Now released, no longer held prisoner, and now he can be at peace.

They said they felt bad, but stood fast, blaming things on him.

Said he should have told us! Got help for it… or maybe counselling!

When the truth remained, if he had, would they have cared one bit?

When all they did, was concoct new evils to commit.

They now carry on regardless, now a new victim they must find.

So, someone is soon to be in danger from this ignorance, so unkind!

Remember, life changes for all; it never stays the same.

Could turn badly on you too. Could YOUR heart withstand such pain?

...In the eye of the beholder!

Wish upon a star

When you wish upon a star,
Your dreams and hopes, may not be so far.

But maybe also plan and plot...
Construct your future with life's finest building blocks.

Contemplation

Uninhibited

SENSUALITY

Seduction is an art form, helps to capture a mate.

Eager, your heart pounding, as your pupils dilate.

Natural attraction burns the desire deep within.

Sexual urges make you rampant, kissing and caressing begin.

Unreserved, you don't hold back; let your loins lead the way.

Animal attraction, the intrigue, gets you clammy as you play.

Lustfully you gaze, as you explore each other's contours.

Injections of lust pumping fiercely as you continue to explore.

Tantalising, the intensity of this new romance grows steady!

Yearning for more sexual encounters, aroused again, you're ready!

My mind

My mind is all a-jumble… I am so confused!
Tests of my faith and mental strength, have all been overused.

Like being spun around, fast, on a roundabout… I struggle to hold on.
My face pulled to distortion, fearing what next will go wrong.

Can't time just stop, hold still, and permit me to catch up?
Maybe, make better choices for my future and clear my past mistakes up.

But life is not that willing, and my request… overruled.
Damn and blast it! Why is it that life must be so very cruel?

My body and mind so numb. Unless things slow down, I can't deal…
…With these tortuous problems that cocoon me, and just won't heal.

Insults, abuse, loneliness, no confidence, no self-belief and no self-worth.
What a cocktail… a true concoction for self-destruction. Man, I feel like dirt!

I ask my guardian angel and those who watch over me…
Help me! Protect me! Keep me safe! Please be there for me?

Stressed to the bone… I feel everyone wants so much of me!
Can't decide just quite what, who or even where I am supposed to be.

It would only take the right person… the right words… the right support…
To help me turn my life around, instead of being so distraught!

Scribble, scrabble, apple

Jasmine

New puppy

I bought myself a puppy.
She is four months and a day.

Beautiful, tiny little thing,
Jasmine is her name.

But what have I let myself in for?
Oh no, what's that on my floor?

A smelly, steamy heapy!
Oh, my goodness... there's some more!

She saturated my favourite rug...
With fragrance 'eau de pee pee'.

She's chewed all my kid's shoes,
Chewed everything, blissfully!

She dragged her bum on my carpet,
In front of my revolted guests.

I could have died of the embarrassment,
...Got her quickly down the vets!

Enjoying our lovely supper,
Her flatulence reeked through the house.

I've had enough, taking her back tomorrow!
The dirty little louse!

But I melt, I can't stay mad,
Look at her adorable, loving eyes.

She tilts her head to the left,
Raises her ear, whimpering... she cries.

Hooked... I'm caught... I took the bait,
Her puppy charm reeled me in.

Despite all of those ones and twos,
I'm keeping my little Jasmine.

She now barks, to go to the toilet,
Sits, rolls over, and holds out her paw.

I wouldn't be without her now,
She's changed with etiquette galore!

She has been such a pleasure,
Turned out to be one of my best friends.

She loves me so unconditionally,
She'll be loyal until the end.

Say 'Arrghrrr!'

Give my ears a break!

Stop your whingeing and whining!
Please, it is driving me insane!

Why won't you talk… not lose your mind?
What must our neighbours think?

You just won't stop your nagging!
Keep polluting all my space.

Attacks my nervous system,
It makes my right eye twitch!

Yet you carry on regardless,
You just love to have a moan.

Not even taking a breather,
When I am on the bloody phone!

Your constant belly aching,
Come on, it needs to stop.

Basically, I don't need it,
I have simply had ENOUGH!

I don't like ultimatums, no!
But feel that there's great need.

So, if you don't stop your moaning,
I'll be gone in hasty speed!

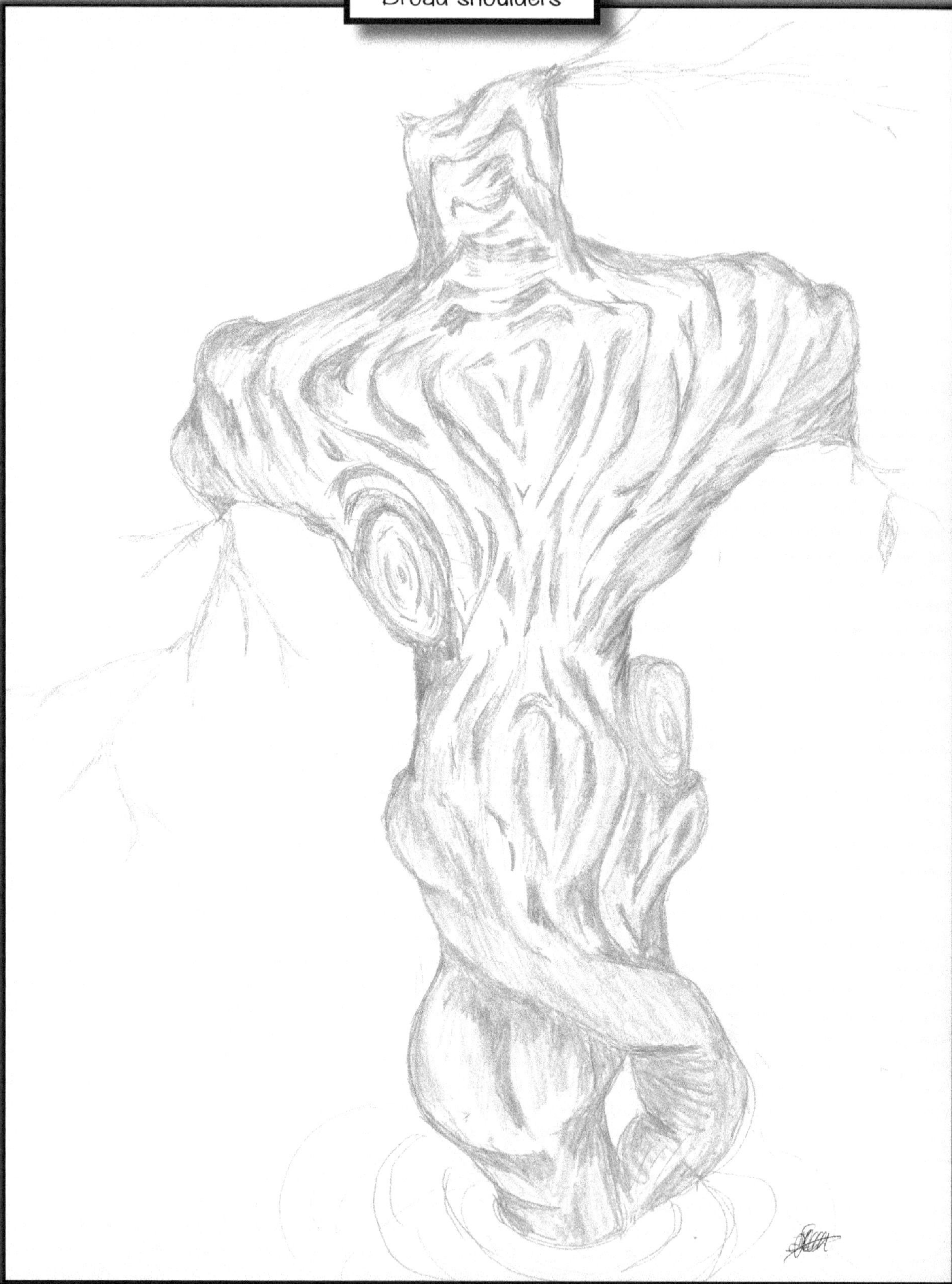

Just jammin'

Big foot

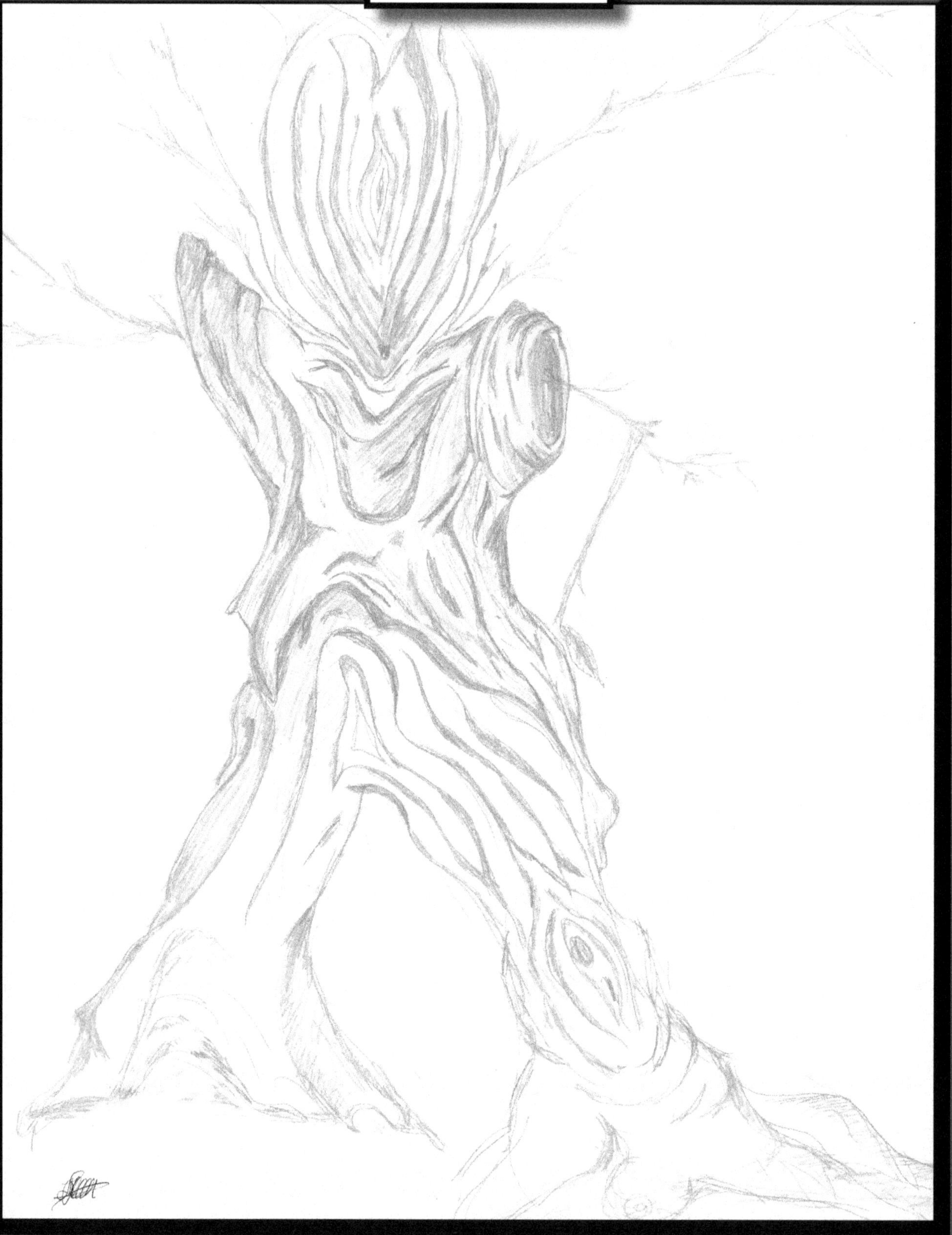

Go girl!

I hear you.

You guide me.

You are my world.

You ground me.

U n c o n d i t i o n a l l y . . .

And when my heart is heavy...

you support me.

That's my family!

An unbreakable link

Freel

The Shyness Anchor

My shyness submerges me… anchoring me to the basin of the sea.
Small bubbles it permits me to breathe… But is it trying to drown me?

I pull, I struggle… but the chain of this anchor holds firm to my limbs.
Won't allow me to be free… won't allow me to swim.

I'm tired of swaying, moving around in this tide.
…battered around in its fierceness, I collide.

Wait, is that the key for these chains that floats before me?
If I use it to unlock these chains… will I truly be freed?

No! Another mirage… my wishful thinking!
My mind, playing tricks… It just keeps teasing!

Oh, to be free… float to the surface… feel the sun on my face.
Be rescued by those who wish to learn of my plight…
My fate.

Then joyous, I will arrive… on a beautiful island, my rescuers and me.
In step we walk, first on sand, then on the firmness of land… goodbye, sea.

A bond we form, of respect, kindness and having good fun.
Then, I could be free to join in… just like everyone.

Go on... take the bait!

Child so contrary

His mum drops him off at a quarter past eight.

She tears off fast, leaving dust in her haste.

He stumbles, trips, crashes clumsily into the room,

He grins oblivious, as I watch on in great gloom.

Menacing expression, embarrassed? He is not,

As he reaches his finger up, to dig out his green snot.

His finger, right up there, altering the shape of his nose.

Then looks up at me laughing, wiping the slime down his clothes.

They sit for a story, he lets one rip on the rug,

The fumes from his fluctuance kills a passing bug.

In the garden, fresh air, as he decides to poo,

Which dripped down his leg, all the way to the loo.

We then made four robots, each kid they did try,

Then painted them nicely and left them to dry.

That menacing child tore those robots to bits.

My nerves now frayed and teeth firmly grit!

What was left of the robots made the other three cry,

This was only a torso, two legs and one gluey eye.

That morning he showed no compassion for my little Tweet,

Who keeled over in his cage, upturned were his feet.

The other poor children cried for the poor little bird,

Who was once perched on his stick singing songs in great word.

No instead, he grabbed his tummy and cried laughing, you see,

Even suggested that we have little Tweety for tea.

Running around screeching, he was causing great mayhem.

Stressed to the bone now, I tried in vain to control him.

Stop spitting, don't throw that, and leave that alone!

Leave her, give that back, that's not nice – put down my phone!

But would he stop doing naughty things?

...If only this were so.

Well, he had to go home..

...as I had, NO control!

Swearing, disgusting, a real filthy tongue,

No discipline instilled in this child so young.

His mother was called, to collect her misbehaving child.

Her reaction to his disgraces, I felt were rather too mild.

She gave him sweeties, can you believe? Despite all he had done!

I wanted to add, "What a fine way of rebuking your son."

She then dragged him away, him still scratching his bum,

Cried a few crocodile tears for her... then turned to me poking his tongue.

Phobia… irrational

Why do clouds and fog scare me?

No one seems to understand, you see.

People do laugh and say that I am mad.

They don't seem to realise… I agree, it's sad!

The phobia manifested at a very young age,

It's getting worse over time as I become more engaged.

In fog, when I was younger, my mother would come and get me,

Guide me home, my eyes sealed, I couldn't bear to see!

Now I'm older my partner has adopted her role,

Thank you both, for understanding, and saving my soul.

I will try to describe in words just how I feel,

When faced alone, oh my goodness…! with my fear to deal.

Yes, it is partly due to its sheer magnitude,

But this is not the main reason why I try to elude.

It appears to some beautiful, glorious in its breadth.

To me it is airy and scary, half terrifying me to death.

It seems so unfair to know that others do not share,

The irrational way my mind seems to adhere.

My heart pounds away thinking of colliding with fog,

Driving through it, it hangs over as we drive pass the bogs.

Hands sweating, tears flowing, I shudder… tightly close my eyes.

My partner, calmly and reassuringly, takes over and drives.

Clouds to me look gigantic and seem weird,

Light and patchy, thick, and dark, they can look angry and fierce.

They are used in airy moments in films, which does not help,

To concentrate the mind, make anticipation and fear, more felt.

Clouds to me seem spiritual and hide more than they reveal,

However, I don't wish to know, more of the dark's secrets, concealed.

Why can I not accept that clouds and fog will always be there?

And handle their presence without any care?

It's crazy to think they would float downwards to get me,

But that's how I feel, and nothing can console me.

Wispy, fluffy, or heavy with rain,

It just doesn't matter, they all affect me the same.

I know that clouds are formed from condensation,

Friends try to describe, with rationalisation.

I wait anxiously to be cured, from this disease so ludicrous,

And live my life restored, fearless, and stand victorious!

It seems impossible, at the moment, to imagine such success,

As clouds and fog are winning their fight to keep me distressed!

Well, you laugh first, old scary clouds,

Cos one day, I WILL, laugh last... ALOUD!

Love is to us

Love is to us, the tender feeling of warmth...
Expressing deep emotions, kindness and thought.

Love is to us, like the ocean, deep as our hearts.
Like the four seasons, our qualities, divided in parts.

Love is to us, the reason for fighting our way through,
To achieve what we feel is important to do.

Love is to us, passion, yet resentment and fear.
Leaving our loved one, whilst wanting them near.

Love is to us, the reason for getting over pain.
Banishing turmoil to feel happy again.

Love is to us, about honesty and being able to forgive.
Important in life, which can be so short-lived.

Love is to us, having a shoulder to cry on.
Support, understanding and someone you can rely on.

Love is to us, about listening and being heard when conversing.
To construct the foundations which build happy living.

Love is to us, saying sorry when you know you are wrong.
Hurt is a feeling that should not be prolonged.

Love is to us, like the flight of two beautiful doves,
Blissfully flying, together in love.

Love is to us, the sensation of happiness when we are together.
Which is why we promise to cherish each other, in marriage, forever.

Love's chase

Oh... to be a wise old owl!

LOVE FONT

‘I love you’
‘…And I love you too.’

‘But you are white!’
‘…and you are, black!’

‘Indeed, we are just text, in love…’
‘Yes! Typed in “Love font…”

‘Let us marry our words together…’
‘Agreed! Let us be… BOLD.’

‘But some other fonts won’t like it.’
‘Wonder if they’ve even given it a go?’

‘My font’s more rich now I share it with you.’
‘In harmony… as one… let us try with the caps lock on too.’

‘AT THE END OF THE DAY WE ARE ONLY JUST WORDS.’
‘NO DIFFERENCE, REGARDLESS OF FONT TYPE, SIZE, COLOUR OR VERB.’

‘JUST LOOK AT US JOINED TOGETHER.’
‘COMPLETING EACH OTHER’S SENTENCES IN VERSE.’

‘SO WONDERFUL, SO HAPPY!’
‘FEELINGS… SO INTENSE, WE COULD BURST!’

‘TOGETHER, WE FLOW AND IT’S SUCH A DELIGHT.’
‘US INTWINED IN TEXT IS A BIT OF ALRIGHT.’

‘BUT, HAVE WE GONE TOO FAST IN BEING SO CAREFREE?’
‘AS IT LOOKS LIKE THE CAPS LOCK HAS SLIPPED… AND WE HAVE TYPED…’

A baby

'I will sit.'

Life: 'I have been looking for you!'

Me   'Why?'

Life: 'Because it is your turn.'

Me: 'But, I am not ready.'

Life: 'Well... that's too bad!'

Me: 'Should I be afraid?'

Life: 'That's up to you!'

Me: 'What should I do? sit or stand?'

Life: 'What do YOU want to do?'

Me: 'I will sit for now... later, maybe, I will stand.'

Life: 'Then, here you go!'

Me: 'Wait! Can I get back to me?'

Life: To get back, go forwards.'

Me: '...it's happening! **Hwuuuuuuuuuuuuuughraaa!**'

I've got YOU!

How I feel

I sit here amongst others, but my mind is so far away.
I laugh and make jokes, but still thoughts of you rain!

At first, we all felt your presence with us so strong.
But now it seems you have had to go, sadly move on.

Where are you, dad? We can't bear that you are no longer near.
Talk to you regardless; but we need to know you can hear.

We really do understand the cycle of life.
But of course, when it happens, it still cuts like a knife.

I look at the clouds, sometimes they form into your face.
Is it your way to reassure me you are with us, there is no empty space?

Told of your passing, in screams of terror down the phone.
My heart pounding heavy, as I had already assumed you had gone.

I sobbed, screamed then lay confused, scared and still.
I watched the full moon numbly, beaming back, lighting my windowsill.

The worst news of my life I had **ever** received.
Wish it was a dream I could wake up from, then the news I could leave.

We flew over to be with Mum, I had to confront all my worst fears,
Of flying, of clouds, heights, your death, it was really hard to bear!

Mum's face, when we arrived to lend our support,
Was so weary and sunken, she looked lost and distraught.

I was scared, I won't lie, for me to go see you in the mortuary.
I didn't think I could bear to come; it was torturous for me!

Cold was your body, as you lay there at rest,
But it was YOU, Dad; you seemed to put all my fears to rest.

We held you, we cried, rubbed your face and arm.
Dear Dad, you changed for us, from cold to warm.

We are adamant that day that we saw you raise a smile,
But we had to leave you there, we had only been given a short while.

At your funeral, it was grim as reality had set in,
Distraught were we in the church, when it all had to begin.

Couldn't accept that the hearse was really carrying OUR dad.
The funeral, people dressed respectfully and mourning, were all for YOU, Dad!

As we sat and sang solemnly through your sermon,
Childhood memories flashed fast through our minds, one by one.

Your casket now opened, we walked to you screaming your name,
Hugged you tightly, we couldn't let go, we were dragged off you in pain.

Still not believing the truth, clear now and in front of me,
That it was really your funeral that we were there to see.

Watching on as the last shovel of earth fully covered your casket.
My heart sank deep within, pulling down my soul like a lead-filled basket.

They sang, placed flowers, danced round your grave as we sat there.
Beautiful flowers, they were, candles lit amongst them twinkling in the air.

We stood on the hill where you lay until it turned dusk.
Heads bowed with our thoughts, still crying, not a word shared between us.

Buried right next to your father up on the hill,
Also, very close to your mother, how proud you must feel.

You got your wish of resting place and there you will remain.
Not in England, in the cold, where you will never walk again.

We cherish your pictures and fond memories of you.
That's all we have left now; we have learnt to cherish each other more too.

People think we should be back to normal because we smile, or it shouldn't be long.
There is no way, Dad, we are empty; they could not be more wrong!

For when it's not my eyes crying, it's my heart deep with the pain.
I would give just about anything to hug you again.

You died a week before your birthday, one month before you were due back,

Two days after your son's birthday. Reminders are not lacked.

We have dreamt of you since, you look happy, beautiful, real nice.

Sometimes I'm sure I hear your voice, offering silent advice.

Mum arrived at the airport alone, wish it could have been with you.

What should have been a happy event, your children a year without you.

You were silent, never told us of the extent of your pain,

You protected us from that knowledge… you never complained.

My memory of our last conversation, you kept saying, "I'm okay!"

I wish you really were, then you would be still here today!

People who knew you, remember you sitting on your wall.

It's a memory which will be held by everyone, forever, a kind of memorial.

It was your time to go, so we must stop thinking of what could have been done.

We will try accepting one day, God's decision.

Please be happy and at peace but accept it when we are sad.

We will move on in time, through the hardest times we have ever had.

I cry tears for you always, I am not sure when they will stop.

Because we so miss you, Dad, and we still love you lots! x

Life: 'I have been looking for you!'

Me: "Hello again, Life. I knew that you would be back at some point. Well, this time I

am more prepared... So, **I will stand!**"

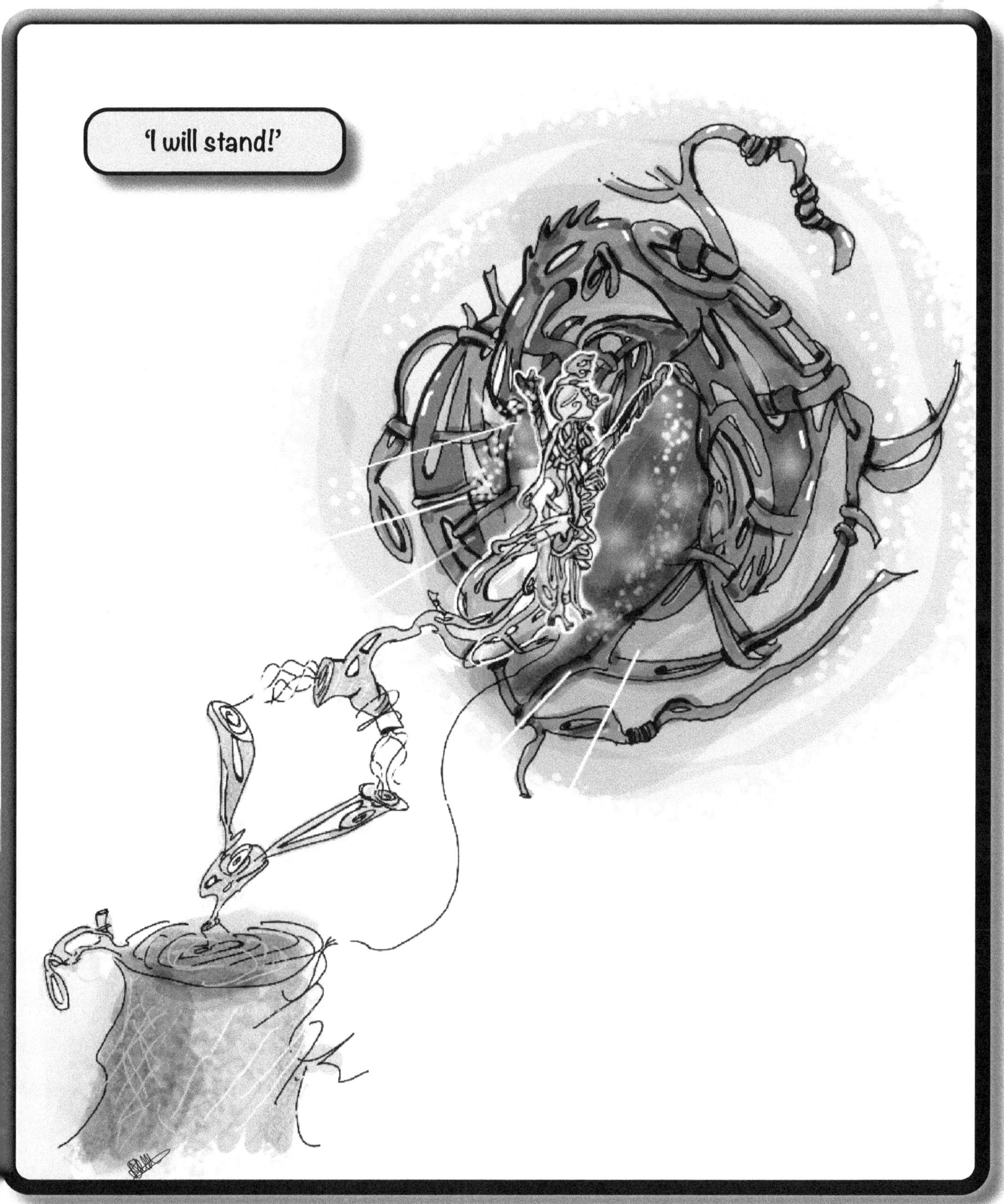
'I will stand!'

A life unfinished... yet wonderfully incomplete!

Troubled by troubles?
How troublesome.

Sometimes I get to put them away before they burst.

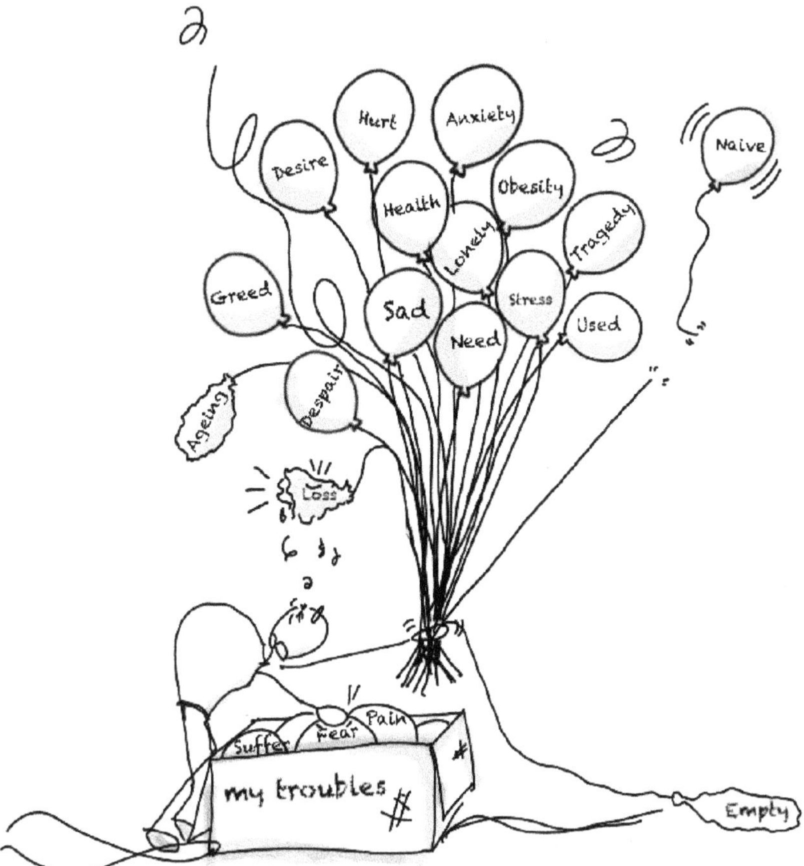

...just take one balloon at a time...

Uplifted...

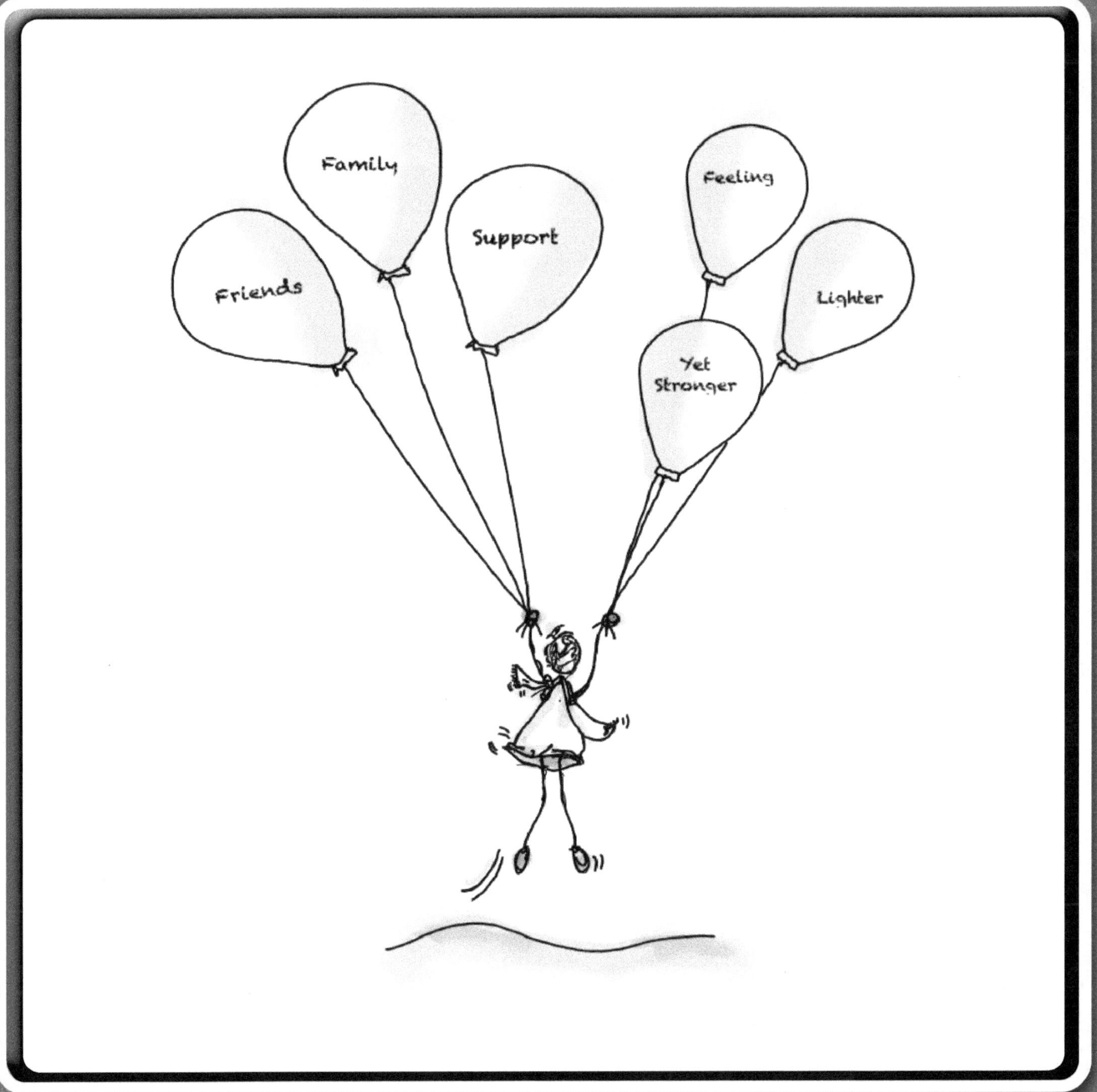

Family
Friends
Support
Feeling
Lighter
Yet
Stronger

Resilience... Life's lifeline!